This Boxer Books paperback belongs to

. . . .

www.boxerbooks.com

For Evgenia Barinova
M.B.

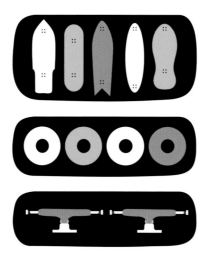

First published in paperback in Great Britain in 2012 by Boxer Books Limited
www.boxerbooks.com

The illustrations were prepared digitally by the author.
The text is set in Adobe Garamond Regular.

ISBN 978-1-907967-43-6

1 3 5 7 9 10 8 6 4 2

Printed in China

All of our papers are sourced from managed forests and renewable resources.

GNARBUNGA

Written and illustrated by
Matthew Bromley

Boxer Books

One day, Gnarbunga appeared from a mucky, messy hole in the ground.

Gnarbunga was made from icky, sticky sludge!

Gnarbunga's icky, sticky sludge got all over the children.

And they loved it!

Some people were
not so happy to get icky,
sticky sludge on them.

Some people didn't mind.
They were a little icky,
sticky and sludgy already.

But some people
got **very** annoyed!

Gnarbunga needed some ideas.

So Gnarbunga found something to do, and this excited him very much.

Gnarbunga needed some

help getting started ...

Gnarbunga had to choose

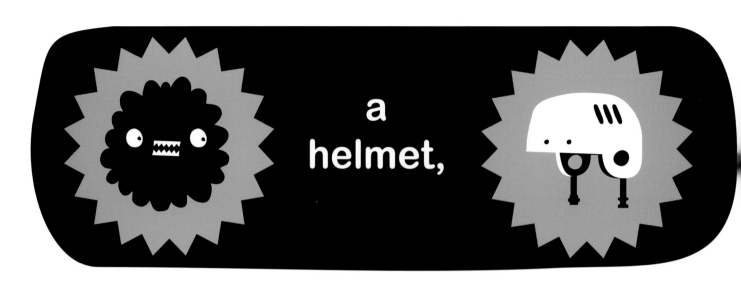

a
helmet,

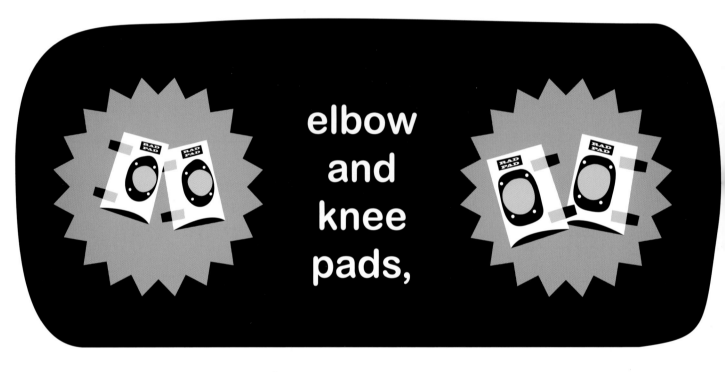

elbow
and
knee
pads,

and
shoes
and
socks.

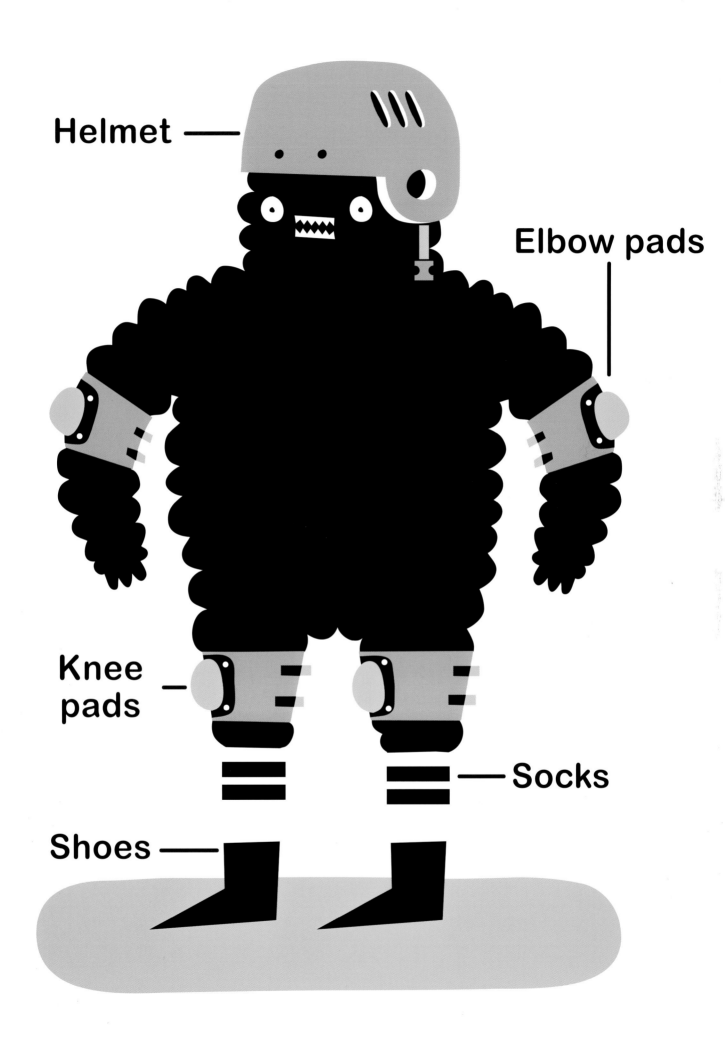

Helmet

Elbow pads

Knee pads

Socks

Shoes

Gnarbunga also had to choose

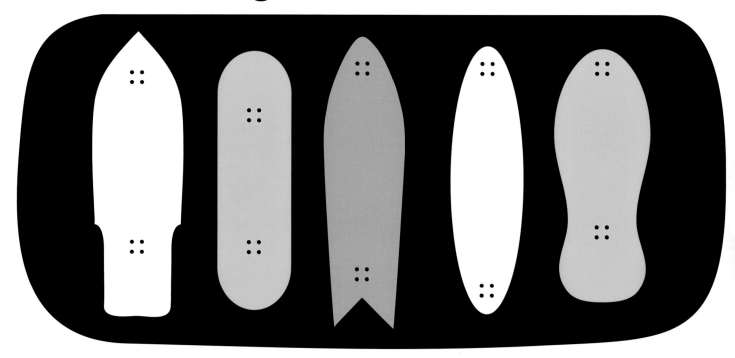

a deck,

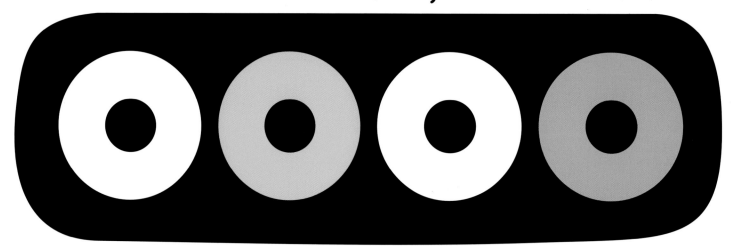

some wheels,

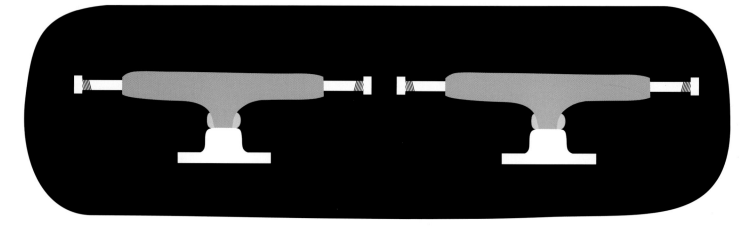

and some trucks!

Gnarbunga got padded up and was ready to go.

He said sorry to the people who didn't like getting icky, sticky and sludgy.

Gnarbunga loved skateboarding.

Gnarbunga learnt the best tricks.

He could kick-flip over a cat ...

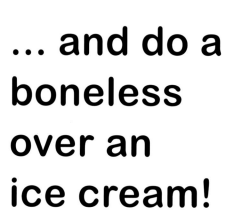

... and do a boneless over an ice cream!

Gnarbunga could even do inverts,
which made everyone shout …

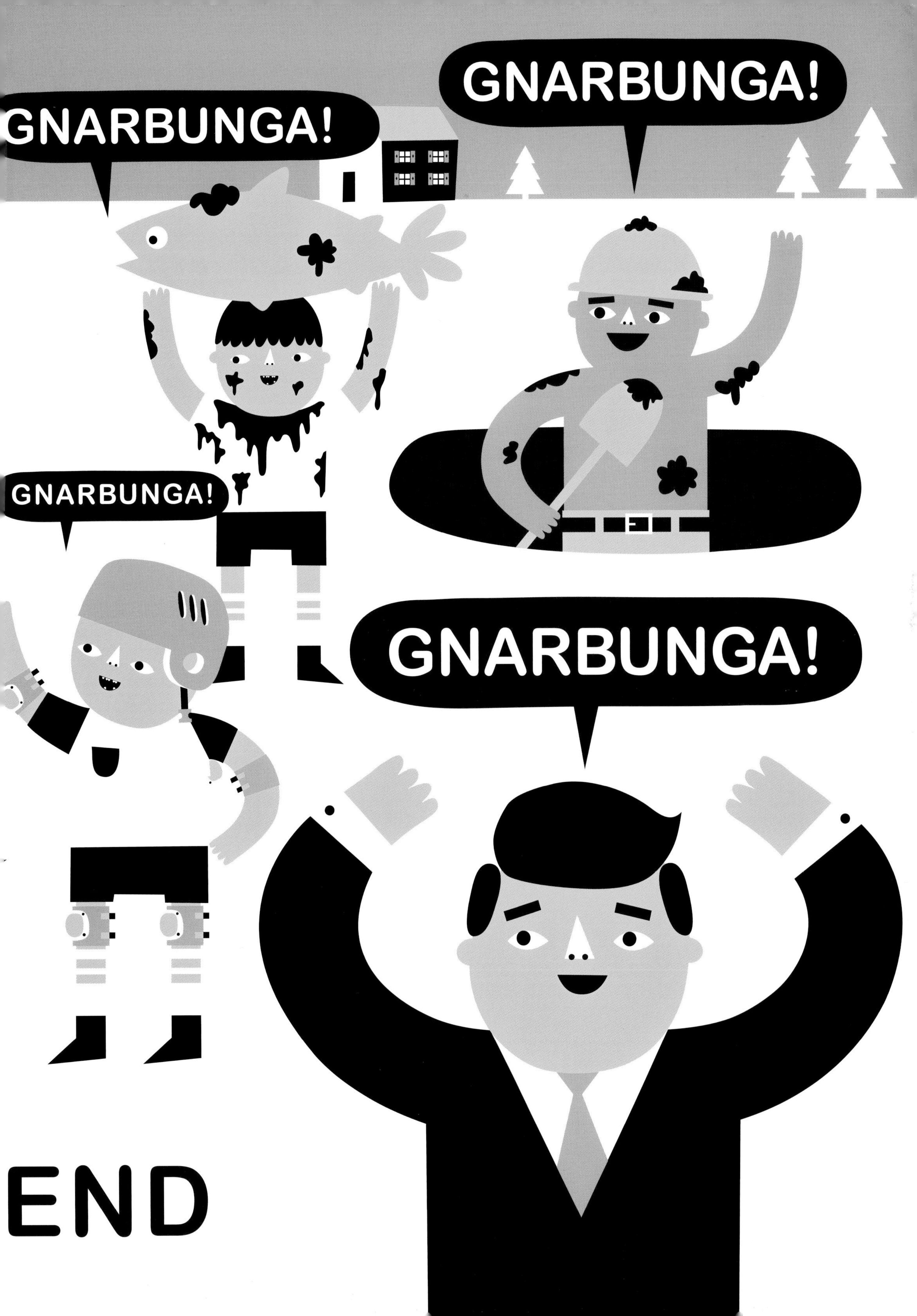
GNARBUNGA!
GNARBUNGA!
GNARBUNGA!
GNARBUNGA!
END

More Boxer Books to enjoy

I Love My Daddy and *I Love My Mummy* • Sebastien Braun

Simple, moving words and beautiful illustrations capture the special bond between parent and child in these stunning titles from Sebastien Braun. *I Love My Mummy* and *I Love My Daddy* are celebrations of parenthood for every mother, father and child.

I Love My Daddy
ISBN 978-0-954737-39-9

I Love My Mummy
ISBN 978-0-954737-36-8

Fine As We Are • Algy Craig Hall

Fine As We Are is an exquisitely illustrated story of sibling rivalry. Little Frog is living happily with his mum until the arrival of a multitude of little brothers and sisters. How will he learn to cope?

ISBN 978-1-905417-74-2

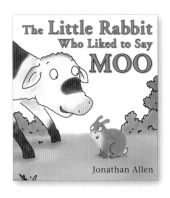

The Little Rabbit Who Liked to Say Moo • Jonathan Allen

Little Rabbit likes to say, "Moo", but Calf points out, "You're not a cow." Soon, Little Rabbit gets the other farmyard animals to join in with their favourite noise. Moo, baa, oink, hee-haw, and quack along to Jonathan Allen's delightful illustrations.

ISBN 978-1-905417-80-3

Duck & Goose • Tad Hills

Duck and Goose find an egg. "Who does it belong to?" they ask. Duck says it is his because he saw it first. Goose says it is his because he touched it first. Little by little, they agree that the most important thing is to look after the egg and decide to share it. Parents everywhere will recognise this tale of one-upmanship, which firmly establishes the positive aspects of learning to share.

ISBN 978-1-905417-26-1

www.boxerbooks.com